October

1 ✗

7 ✗ 8 ✗

14 ✗ 15 ✗

21

A Birthday for Cow!

JAN THOMAS

Houghton Mifflin Harcourt

Boston   New York

www.hmhco.com

The illustrations in this book were done digitally.

ISBN: 978-0-544-85002-6

Manufactured in China
SCP 10 9 8 7 6 5 4 3 2 1
4500700828

For Will

Today is Cow's birthday...

Yippee!

Pig and Mouse are going to make Cow the best birthday cake EVER!

CAKE?!

They put
flour and
sugar and
eggs in
a big bowl.

Next, they
mix it with…

Then they put it in the oven.

Can a TURNIP go in, TOO?

And they ice the cake, and on top they put...

I know!

Is that what I think it is? This is the best birthday EVER...

Sometimes I brush my teeth using a turnip.

Get your child ready to read in three simple steps!

**1** **I READ**	Read the book to your child.
**2** **WE READ**	Read the book together.
**3** **YOU READ**	Encourage your child to read the book over and over again.

Looking for more laughs?

Don't miss these other adventures
from Jan Thomas:

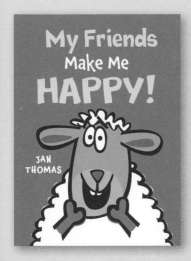

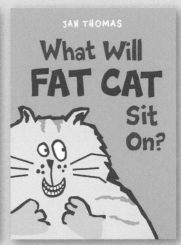

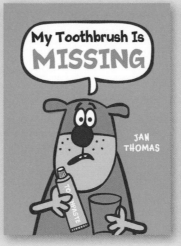